Yes, Please!

written by Pam Holden
illustrated by Pauline Whimp

We like the taste of juice.

We like the taste of fruit.

We like the taste of meat.

We like the taste of salad.

We like the taste of fish.

We like the taste of vegetables.

We like the taste of rice.

We like the taste of cheese.